<u>Too, *River*</u>

By
Stanley Alexander MARTIN

Copyright 2008, Nana baBa jaH-aYe
ISBN: 978-0-9559904-3-4

Dedicated to all males…

This text was first published in "DEATH OF THE GOD", sponsored by MIND and THE MILLENIUM COMMISSION....

Mythics contents Form

"0". Mythics..........................

(Innocence "Before")
(i)
(he hid the nakedness from Him because he was "Aware")
(he kneweth "his nakedness" with Him because he was "conscious")
("I")
("the-I die")

1.   Preface on dub-poetry...

2.   Blues of the Flesh..........
   Love story set in a
   pop music tradition

Glossary of Patois..........................

3.   The River......................
   Love story set in a
   classical music tradition

4.   Anima Rising................
   The last two days
   of the Christ, retold
   to classical rhythms

"0": the utterance of/at nothingness..."The Word"

2. Form Mythics content
(after Vladimir Propp)

(Equilibrium):
Dis-equilibrium:
Search ---->
Re-equilibrium:
(Wedding celebration)...

3. Contents mythics form

Journey to Life's fulfilment, and...

4. The neUn

Equilibrium:	","
/	refers,
/	and
v	1 is, and
Wedding:	defers.
etc., etc...	and 2 relates, and...
	referral/deferral...

5. neUn maths

"0"	:	1 &
1 &	:	1 x 1/1 + 1
1 x 1/1 + 1	:	2 &.... : ...infinity &

6. neUn consciousness

neGus :	sleeping
neAus :	awakening
neXus :	connecting ----> *thinking*
	researching
	translating
neYin :	the loss at *rising to* One
neXus :	enlightenment...

neXus-neGus :   *the sleep after enlightenment rising to* Too*... etc., etc...*

7. One relates to *Too*
(after Standard English)

One knows the excellence of *no*-thing in all things: the tribute of the River;

Someone holds the keys:
Anyone can the further stairs, and scent the Heaven sent;
Everyone has the dream:
All-of-one knows

god: *God* is almighty;

Here a *Person* speaks

To *Child*:

is *Unborn* to

The *Spirit* awakening...

Love is the inner winding chords to *Too*: *soul*:

the *Real* is *Sure*, *Certain*: *Concrete*....

8. Mythic Structures

i. Form/Content
(after Ferdinand de Saussure)

$$\text{Signifiers} \quad - \quad \begin{array}{c} \text{"0"} \longrightarrow 1 \\ 4 : 5! \ / \\ 3 \longleftarrow 2 \end{array} \quad : \text{"TOO"}$$

ii. Form contents Mythics
(after Claude Levi-Strauss: Greek myths being structures of how to form "2" from "1")

i.

Greek Myths $F\ x \quad : \quad F\ y \ \sim \ F\ a \quad : \quad F\ Y$
$\qquad\qquad\qquad a \qquad\qquad b \qquad\quad x \qquad\qquad a{-}1$

Greek Myths: $\mathbf{A} = F\ (x) : \quad F\ (Y) \ \sim \quad \mathbf{B} = F\ (b): \quad F\ (Y)$
$\qquad\qquad\qquad a = -(i^2){:}i^4 \quad b = i^2{:}{-}(i^4) \qquad\quad x \qquad\qquad a-1$
Translates.... $\qquad 1/{-}1{:} \quad -1/1 \quad \sim\underline{(1+1/1x1)}{:} \ -2/2{:} \qquad$ "0"/"0"

Which translates: "Functions of one and its contradiction, is *transformed* into two, contradicting the Word which is God", e.g., contradicting functions $Y = -x\ ; x = -Y$......

    A man and a woman contradict and are *transformed* into a union of **too** (**light or dark**), in a contradiction with the forces of the WORD which is God... For example, Adam and Eve in Eden...

ii.

"Too" Myths: $\mathbf{A} = F\ (x) : \quad F\ (Y)\ \sim\ \text{"Too"} = F\ \underline{(i^2){:}{-}(i^4)}{:} \quad F\ \underline{(Y)/\text{"1"}}$
$\qquad\qquad\qquad -(i^2){:}i^4 \quad i^2{:}{-}(i^4) \qquad\qquad\quad x \qquad\qquad\quad -x/i^2$

Which translates: "Functions of One and its contradiction, is *transformed* into two contradicts to it = Too", e.g., contradicting functions $Y = x + 1; x = Y-1$, which yields:
$\qquad\qquad\qquad 1/{-}1 \quad : \qquad \text{"0"/"0"} \quad \sim \quad x^2{:}\underline{i^2/1^2{:}1+1/1x1}{:}{-}2{:} \quad -2$

    A good man contradicts with the forces of the WORD and are *transformed* into a union of **too** in a contradiction with another union of **too**... For example in the Bible when chosen man Adam forms a union with Eve, and their too is contradicted by the too of the field...

iii.

River Myths: $\mathbf{C} = F\ (B = (x^3 + 1)) : F\ (Y^3 {-}1) \ \sim\ \mathbf{River} = \mathbf{D} = F\ (i^3){:}F\ (Y^3 - 1)$
$\qquad\qquad\qquad -i^3 \qquad\qquad i^3 \qquad\qquad\qquad\qquad (x^3+1) \quad i^3$

Which translates: "Functions of Too and its contradiction, is *transformed* into a discourse of Eight, in a contradicts to the WORD ", e.g., contradicting functions $Y = x^3 + 1; x = Y^3-1$, which yields:
....**"Too"** = $-2{:}{-}B = 2 \qquad \sim \qquad$ **River** = $6+2i{:}8+: \quad i^3 = i^2 = i^3(1-(i^4)) =$ "0"

    A union of **too** in a contradiction with another union of **too**... are *transformed* into the relay of a discoursive fractal of eight, which contradict the WORD... *The Too of Adam and Eve, yielded a discoursive fractal, or* **River**, *in later tales of Noah,*

Abraham, Lot, Moses, David, Solomon, Jesus Christ, Mohammed, and Yogi Singh....

iii. Form content Mythics
(after Roland Barthes)

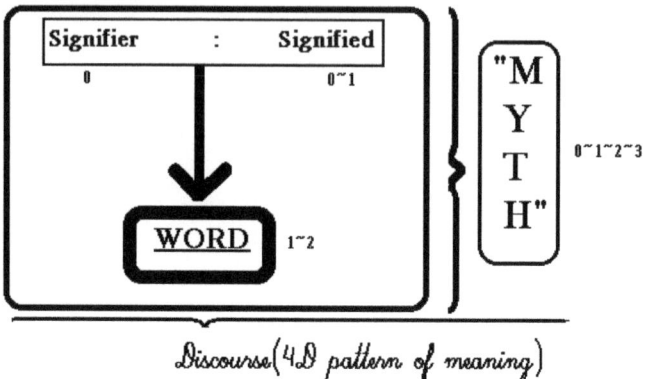

1--->   A *Signifier* defers to the floating utterance of nothingness ("0")...
2--->   A *Signifier* always makes a referral to itself of a *SIGNIFIED*...
3--->   A *SIGNIFIED* has deference to A *WORD* MEANING...
4:      The *WORD* is relayed (referral/deferral!) in the total language as a path to truth, a "lie line": a "*MYTH*"...
5...   Each "*MYTH*" owns a pattern of speech, a "*DISCOURSE*", which is its "*too*"! rhetoric...
... 6. "*Programming*": 7. "*Catalogue*": 8. "*Library*": 8+. "*Web*"....

8+. Go! Mythic translating Alphabet
(after Egyptology)

a		-	sleeping one/thing/"1"
b	-	be/big	
c	-	caged see	
d	-	do	
	e	-	awake one/the spirit-in-the-thing/he, she, it
	ee	-	*aware one/consciousness/"I"*
f	-	force/sign bad	
g	-	sign good/vehicle	
h	-	home/heaven	
	i	-	aware one/thinking one/consciousness/"I"
j	-	just/joy	
k	-	know	
l	-	here	
m	-	move	
n	-	negatively top/black chief	
	o	-	connecting one/matter/"0"
	oo	-	linking one/person/"you"
p	-	take it/leave	
q	-	give it/stay	
r	-	presently/are	
s	-	understanding	
t	-	the way/money	
	u	-	linking one/person/"you"
v	-	too/two	
w	-	route	
x	-	connecting/suffering	
	y	-	conscious one/soul/"why"
z	-	end	

Letters joining-up add "to" in their middle:
e.g., "oo" = "connecting one to connecting one"
            = "**one** connecting one"
            = "linking one".

Letters join-up to make words,
e.g., "book" = "be to linking one to know"
              = "be you know"

"The River" means:
   "The way heaven/home presently aware one of too to sleeping one present"....

1. Preface on duB-poetry

The term *dub-poetry*, meaning "poetry with a musical rhythm", usually reggae rhythms, was coined in the 1970's by dub-poet. Oku Onoura; the genre had already been explored by Linton Kwesi Johnson and John Cooper Clarke in Britain, and others in Jamaica.

The roots of dub-poetry lies in the Jamaican DJ's like I-Roy and Big Youth, and comes from a tradition of poetry set to music harking back to the Last Poets, in the United States, Beat Poets in the 1950's and 1960's. As a form, dub-poetry is a survival through slavery of the African praise poets, the *Griots*, who used songs to their kings and others in the culture, and acted as folk historians.

As praise poets, the dub-poets were journalistic spokespersons for the common folk, and spoke up about news events in the history of the culture they lived in, giving praise or curse accordingly.

Nowadays, a derivative of the griot-style, rap, is commonplace, but most commonly, with the political stance not always there, the rappers boasting, or talking grandly of themselves...

Dub-poetry dealing with the politics of personal relationships is not too common, and is the essential feature of this book, especially in *The River* and *Blues of the Flesh*. I have taken some of the rhythms too, away from much of their traditional bases and into the classical genre...

                                                      Stanley Alexander Martin
                                                              January 2008

4.   Blues of the Flesh
**Love story set in a
pop music tradition**

1. Pop

And if you are a star, shines
signal, shines as a sun, shines
not as you are, shines
light years away in the distance, shines
without par; shines in the past,
makes you bleed light eternal, you can't be dark:
yet you can be darker,
darker than you are:

so tell, tell me how
stars can be so much of everything, tell
me how you pay to shine
eternally, become a star,
how stars start;
and how stars fade away...

Can't face the truth about the day;
day's break
day's distance into dark, day's
clouds, and day's
rain along the way, a day
away, day's
sun garages in its park, day dreams,
the sky's altar is a holy dress:

all I can see is stars...

2.   Dub

Cat along low walls raw
he walks, no
cantankerous talk he talks,
a Ewe:
spend no spare words writ wrote for me,
this cat tall Babel downs
to blackboard chalk...

Down the dead darlings dare
he drops, no
beaten brow of head he fops,
a Bantu:
runs rings around a roundabout you,
dedicated head
not buried by copse...

Sing the sound-songs talking
drumbeat, he comes
bass gongs beaten on every feet:
a Rasta:
ears harken laugh to
Africa, the swing
swells sing as past and
future meet...

Tell he tall tale till
trembles truth, mouth
mind; monster might follows
mute:
Yoruba?
Yes! and Ewe, Bantu too, and Rasta!
Lion along low wall walks tall in youth!

3. Reggae

Sidun sidung sidung
long time sun come
sidun sidung
nahm rum.

Gidun, gidung gidung
long time have fun
gidun gidung
ben' dung.

Lidun, lidung lidung
old man nah young
lidun lidung
-soon come!

4. Rock

Come to me sweet sister moon
I am the sun, I sparkle
and I am waiting:
juice me when the night-time comes;
and can you stay with me till tomorrow morning
when the dawn sits dew upon the grass like diamonds:
I shall hang the sky around your shoulders...

My iceberg heart likens to a sieve
through which the cold-water ocean breaks:
can you meet me
like two trains of colliding aches,
knead me like the baker bakes,
hear me like an empty church:
please, please translate,
lover, I await...

A sorrow sits upon me like a hawk
sits upon hot air,
a shadow veils the sun: it's winter
remind me of weathers when it's spring;

and can you lay upon my garden like a hedgerow
brighten my window-sill with flowers;
I shall thank you with a shine of summer...

My shrouded soul likens to a corpse
through which its breathing hesitates;
can you kiss me with the love
a sailor's ocean breaks
arm me with the strength my mother makes:
consider me like your holy book:
please, please relate:
I await...

5. Rap

I'm like a train on rail
a boat on sail
like a fisherman's line,
long gone bait: King Kong
of Empire state...

I'm either in a fever, or seizure, or neither:
grace, what a face! what shall I say?
"Do you love me?"

I stick like a fly
I pin like a bee
I'm high ball
rub-a-dub king: I love you
"Do you love me?"

Grand slam
out with ma'am
-you like my face!
-where's your place!
... O it's hot!
let's take off what's-it-nots...

I'm either in a fever, or seizure, or neither!
Done!
"You've come?"
-What shall I say?
"Do you love me?"

Oops! boops!
too many cooks!
My you're fat!
Why is that?

"... O, I'm pregnant!"
Life jail sentence!

I'm either in a fever, or seizure, or neither!
Strife! I've a wife!
What shall I say?
"Do you love me?"

I stick like a fly, I
pin like a bee: I
love you!

"She loves me!"

6. Ragga

Man goes to blues-dance
man says to woman - yea,
let's go-deh! All night!

I who had the feeling there
I was let down
I who had the feeling there
left with a frown...

Like a journey into Africa,
my tongue became mute
there was a snake out there
playing on a flute

at once my heart sang:
finally with someone:
the tune on the flute was a brute!

But leaning on the temple hall
I knew others had been playing on my wall:
they say this was a place that was sacred!

At this my heart sang:
lost among the throng,
the pace of the place was a race!

I who had the feeling there
I was let down
I who had the feeling there
left with a frown...

We struck oil in the valley
the rhythm made us dance:
joy like needles,
thrusting like a lance:

at once my heart sang,
but the force made cells bang:
the cause of the pause was the laws...

7.   Country Blues

She crazy, she crazy
crazy baby:
pork chop cooking up tonight!
that's right!

I got a woman so rare
I call her my tender roast beef...
I got a woman so rare
I call her my tender roast beef...
she melt like surlion,
like surlion she tastes so sweet!

I brought home my business
laid it out on the kitchen floor...
I brought home my business
laid it out on the kitchen floor...
when I finished working,
I wanted to work some more...

I'm a cook nine-to-five
every evening I'm a chef...
I'm a cook nine-to-five
every evening I'm a chef...
my woman like to eat meat,
one day she's eat us both to death!

Showed her my sausage
she say: "Lord! what a big piece o'pork!"...
Showed her my sausage
she say: "Lord! what a big piece o'pork!"...
I put it in the pot
and praised the God She invented work!

I stirred-fried that sausage
when the juice began to flow...
I stirred-fried that sausage
when the juice began to flow...
that meat got so tender
we practically ate it raw!

My woman vote for Labour
she likes to swell the poor...
My woman vote for Labour
she likes to swell the poor...
when we finished eating
like Oliver she asked for more!

I got a woman so rare
I call her my tender roast beef...
I got a woman so rare
I call her my tender roast beef...
if she don't get second helping
she holla out for thief!

8. Folk

Is birth by-the-way
and is birth wise?
Is that all you say?
"Qu'est-ce-que c'est que sais?"
My love's eyes!

Is life a run-way
and is life prize?
Is that all you say?
"Qu'est-ce-que c'est que sais?"
My love's eyes!

Is death away-day
and is death lies?
Is that all you say?
"Qu'est-ce-que c'est que sais?"
My love's ayes!

9.   Lover's Rock

Galang galang
you always follow fashion!

Ring the rhythm, don't plea caution
me and me woman life at stake
so don't hold rhythm, play dub-plate
Galang galang
you always follow fashion!

Come to blues dance
to jump and prance,
dee-jay him, frighten dance...
mean say, man and woman left pickney
fi dee-jay him
play wit we?
Galang galang
you always follow fashion!

Dash wey the life uptown
flash we Dennis Brown;
please on Gregory Isaacs- else
blues-dance riot!
man and woman come fi rub belly
leave dem pickney watching telly
we married life at stake,
selector me warning you, play dub-plate!
Galang galang
you always follow fashion!

Wa this! Mr Frankie Paul!
Steady Freddie - Lord!
me back against the wall
- mercy mercy selecter
please have mercy!

Selecter selecter, please have mercy!

10. Dub-Poetry

Galang alang yu own pace
galang boy, you is man
an you have a plan:
galang boy!

Bring her sing-ting
sing-ting fi de ring
mek she ring-ding,
she want sing sing-ting!

A wuk yu wuk
you nuh bruk, a wuk yu wuk
a pick up butt
you and she in luck - yu wuk!

Sickly pickney nah dead pickney
dem want wet-knee
dem soon healthy pickney!

A dutti shirt nah dutti!
but e wuti doh dutti boy,
she an yu pickney dem smile ee?
E wuti!

11.   Samba

My love sends the ocean
tidies like a broom the waves:
kilns kisses of devotion to the night
she sits upon the day
and stares away the stars...

My love wears for ringlet the swooning sun
my love is mother-of-pearl the moon - but!

how long shall sunshine shimmer the naked moon
shimmy a shingle of shilling upon the night
shall a shilling of shine surrender to the night
shall night sunshine?

Or shall night shell shelter from a shanty town of stars?

12.   Jazz Rock

Free!
Free!
Free at last!
Freedom, freedom at last!

Freedom is a bird without a heart,
heart-broke from start,
sitting on hot air it floats,
floats without a heart:
to die, to die and depart!

Sitting above heart
no heart clouds my chart
I sit above my chart:

hovering, I start to start,
Start wings beating fast, faster than fast:
windrush thrush,
       thrusting to flush to rush
              downwind seeking clear
gliding on air to hear
       warbling in ear:
is my lover returned here?

Free!
Free!
Free at last!
Freedom, freedom at last!

Freedom is a bird without a heart,
heart-broke from start,
sitting on hot air it floats,
floats without a heart:
to die - and depart!

13. Urban Blues

Flood finding flushing,
flushing fire-flood and fire-storm;
fishing for fishes, fisherman's fright is form...

She could be upstanding,
swell me till day's break strolls along...
She could be upstanding,
swell me till day's break strolls along...
a match to a flame, a flame burning to a mighty sun...

Flood finding flushing,
flushing fighting fire-flood and fire-storm;
fishing for fishes, fisherman's fright is form...

Fine me find me
find my flavour flavouring your tongue - yes!
Fine me find me
find my flavour flavouring your tongue...
future's flight, future's flight has come...

Print paper pretender
print paper passion pretending pain...
pretext pretext!
pain pricks, pain pricks!
plain paper, plain paints pricks
print paper passion, pain is plain...

from my first moment of rising
I work and count the scars,
but each night my woman freed me,
she freed me from my prison bars....

Print paper pretender
print paper passion pretending pain...
pretext pretext!
pain pricks, pain pricks!
plain paper, plain paints pricks
print paper passion, pain is plain...

Drum drummie me heart drum drum,
bass beat by drum
down drum
beat bass by drum
hung drum
done drum!

Flood finding flushing,
flushing fire-flood and fire-storm;
fishing for fishes, fisherman's fright is form...

From a saint to a sinner,
from sinner to a sinner's fall...
From a saint to a sinner,
from sinner to a sinner's fall...
she would lay her cotton on me,
she wear me to the ball...

a man may journey and think,
the train would always come along...
a man may journey and think,
the train would always come along...
when he arrive at the station
the train has long since come and gone.

14.   Afro-Rock

Drum drum drummy
me heart drum drum
hum drum
base beat by drum
hung on drum
dumb drum
done drum...

a welcoming home
welcome home
home from roam,
welcome!
akwaaba! welcoming within!
akwaaba! welcoming within!
akwaaba! welcome to my skin
welcome home to friend,
welcome home my friend...

akwaaba! welcoming within!
akwaaba! welcoming within!
I cannot sing the words
wings have given flight to words:
absurd
catch me, catch me. catch me:
all alone, freedom became a bird
bird-brained bird
gift-less with wings
tied-up with strings
akwaaba! welcoming within!
akwaaba!
welcome home my skin
watch me watch me watch me...
TAKE OFF!

Glossary

a	-	is
akwaaba!	-	welcome!
alang	-	along
ben' dung	-	rave up
blues	-	type of black dance music
bruk	-	broke
dash wey	-	throw away
deh	-	there
dem	-	them
doh	-	though
dub-plate	-	hit record
dutti	-	dirty
e	-	it's
ee	-	yes
fi	-	for
galang	-	go along/I don't believe you
gidun/gidung	-	get down
lidun/lidung	-	lie down
mek	-	make
nahm	-	eat greedily
nah/noh	-	not
pickney	-	child
Qu'est-ce-que c'est que sais?	-	what is it that knows?
ring-ding	-	celebrate
rub-a-dub	-	sexy person
rub-belly	-	Black sexual dance for couples
selecter	-	one who chooses records at dance
sidun/sidung	-	sit down
sing-ting	-	something

wa	-	what
wet-knee	-	spoil
wit	-	with
wuk	-	work
wuti	-	worth it
yu	-	you

1. The River

**Love story set in a
classical music tradition**

River the beginnings

If the storms;
if the clothes wet and I
a rider in your storms:

if I a vehicle in my cruiser to your coast;
lightning bolt crashing to your heart:
shall you under me your umbrella;
shall I a shelter from the rain?

Landlocked the sailor from the shore;
land-sick
and swashbuckling to your door:
the suit wet and I
a thunder in your storms:

if I a passenger in your ship;
lightening into your deck of Queen of Hearts,
shall you suicide me at the rails,
haul me to your keel,
tie me to a knot in your ropes:
or whistle me onto board as Jack of your calling card?

If the storms;
if the sails wet and I
a rider in your storms:
shall I the spring clean and new,
shall night wrap me up in two wells,
shall we warm?
I a rider in your storms....

River at Oxford

Through day-shine waited
dead till dark shared my skin;
electric currents ran through my wire:
through oven waited:
for woman with spark to lend me fire...
I don't lie in bare skin:
you can't hide naked...

Love is church my sacred,
can lie truth love secret?
all through furnace of day I waited...

Day deserted sky,
the full moon crowned its shine,
night hitch-hiked in with traffic of stars;
crazy wondered why
woman-light won't shadow my prison bars:
lover-mine, love must wine
nakedness won't lie...

Let your flesh rescue me
censor celibacy:
all through drunkenness of night I waited...

My foundation tree
is nakedness and you;
flesh is delight bared naked skin to skin;
lover sharing she
it's nakedness my soul wears deep within,
so lover come make two:
make naked free me...

woman-mine come to dine, please my desire
fashion feast from whine
my water make wine
holy in me shine: you would lend me fire!

River at Abingdon

I did dare your highways:
road way where the piston snap
to the wheel-rim crack
on the line where the aqueduct stops:
Did you drive me where the eagle was flying.

I conquered sleep,
who dared to brave the storms:
I came indoors from the rains...

Was I a passenger in her car:
she drove down my thoroughfares
trafficking down my highroads:
from Lands End to John O'Groats:

we coasted down to dreams,
lost in a countryside of sleep....

River at Reading

How to repeat the sweet surrender...

At the first stroke of midnight's was she
rowing into my moorings with a broken dance:
shall my water wine the chance?

How to repeat the sweet surrender?

if river the fine summer shall I winter,
shall she winter shall be winter;
shall be spring if I winter, and
both fall if I to the autumn come...

But as she did spring
the nevers to the autumn fall,
or winter call,
and we took to cruising as the summer season...

River at Henley

Was her riverbanks high
and her waters deep;
she gathered to me the storms of passage;

was I ever landlocked on her course,
coasting to her coast...

Her chalk hills and downs
was garden for the rest upon;
she was rose clinging to the trunk of tree:

was I ever tasting the garden's fruit,
a song on my magic flute...

Her highland fling and belly-dance
brought on the summer's season;
fiddle to the climax of the jig;

was I a sailor's to a sailor's reel,
white flag to masthead.

River at Windsor

Dining on a kiss and dance:
feast for I and my lady,

sleep was breakfast,

lunch
a walk by the water,
river in the rain;

dinner-for-two:
ironing the mattress,

supper:
a cuddle before the fire:

hunger was separation:
work brought hunger-pains...

a meal of our bodies meeting
was food fit for the gods.

River at Kingston

When your clouds have silver lining,
never thunders and lightning,
and the rain is never wet;
and your sky is falling...

A little bird in your chest is dying:
the sky is falling....

when everything tastes of sugar,
arsenic isn't the poison for you,
and gall is laced with gin;
everything tastes sweet...

Your tongue is tied-up in knots:
your senses are falling....

Sitting on a bridge at daybreak,
the tide at low ebb;
the night takes off her nightgown,
dawn strokes her hair...

morning sings in a chorus:
the sun is falling upside-down....

River at Richmond

All along the Riverbank at Richmond:
a high tide greets evening;
a dog walks his girl, and
the pretty preen and pride:
loud along the long walk lingering crowds gather and gawk...
the dog and girl walk back, and:
the doomed day jumps...

The dark night curtsied in and put on her nightdress...

Tender to this night the holding hands is day;
tender to night the returning day:
as all dogs the howl at moon:
bowls a high tide towards another night in gale...

River at Brentford

She's become a crossroad
cross words coming into view:

her secret eyes
wet eyes,
dabbling with a handkerchief
at the nearest spring onion:

ordinary people can have
such ordinary pain....

ordinary pain has move in with me
and I'm a cardigan
back-to-front...

she's become a crossroad
opening up to view:

my closed eyes are opening wider
every day...

I tell you:
"I love you,":

and keep a frightened little bird
clenched to my chest....

River at Kew

Spoken of the green
an island in a child;
the running one river:
and all was nothings in that months of nine,
a shout to the silence in my mother's milk
made "I"...

I spoke of the "me";
declensions in my two fists
fought me up to my father's size:
the world was an airy dale:
that was asleep...

At nineteen
"it" spoke in me between the he and she,
one world went before the small acts
of inner voices:
which awoke...

On a night when the full moon
howled "we" on my fathering bed,
One word saw You, the Other
saw They, mocking in their sleeping pines:
this was an active
man teaching all his moments:
the sounding clock was midnight's:
this creature comfort's was "the-It"
the-It was God's interior silence:
a mirror of me was my two unraveled palms:
all past/future acts bespoken....

River at Chiswick

Where cords the spill electrics,
where the river runs deep,
where comes the metaphysics of the brain,
is the-It;
where moneys manna,
a lie in my sleep,
where spirits haunt the possession of my lids,
and contentment:
the storms of pain and God
breaks no light I like
but the-It gives:
the Ugly is fair,
and Order a beauty beyond the bliss
of this Life
this world,
this presentiment of my soul;
I speak of pressure-dropped,
and the toil of Ideas:
a walk by quiet waters;
a wonder has settled in my lap,
like a purring tiger,
a hawk hung on hot air;
if the release of hunger,
if passion relents,
if I dare to drop disease of work:
to live in Eternal time,
and know that Everything is One with
Everybody and Everyone,
all things come to a fair returns:
I am the living,
I am the-It.

River at Hammersmith

You were tank-top,
I was black and blue,
but no-one makes my size giant,
but you....
when we dance I go to sleep.

You were vanilla ice,
I was panned and tanned,
but no-one drives my car,
but you:
when we dance, I sleep...

You were tasted sweet,
I, incomplete,
I left you by the river:

I took the music for granted:
we fell out dancing....

River at Battersea

A sleep that gathers.
a kiss-me demon-like,
clings my kiting-to-sky back to cords:
same sleep my fathers,
same sleep savage-in-me looking backwards:
Eden snake in psyche:
war-in-me weathers.

It reins me down with rain
and reigns in me the rain:
drown my water sky such stormy weathers.

Dark star eats me: fire!
light as whole sun heavy,
a spot reduces the sun to centre,
gravity pyre:
turns top centripetal to this centre:
heats dungeon interns me:
no thing but desire...

And shall I ever dark?
shall I never spark?
To combust in nova with another's?

To again the fire!
phoenix the fright of flames,
hot scorch with flint the crackling timber,
electric wire,
burn bridges behind such stormy weather,
put to pot-boil the rains:
to again the fire!

So are we hurricane, so prison,
so alive with fever,
so warry all-weather:
so does that sleep gather us out garden.

River at Lambeth

I'm become a cross word
crossroads coming into view:

her darling eyes
are wet eyes,
smooching with a handkerchief
at the merest touch of lips:

ordinary people
ordinary pain....

ordinary pain is with me again
and I'm a straitjacket
tied at the back...

I've become a cross word
opening up to you:

my open eyes are opening wider
every day...

I tell you:
"I need you,":

and a frightened little bird
is dying in my fist....

River at Westminster

I'm skinned to bone;
was my brave bull:
can't find a pound to put in the parcel:
wedding bells tolling the day:
that cash-and-carry religion
they sell it,
you can't afford it;

love prouder than a heavyweight:
hawk! diva a rabbit to be his centrefold...

I'm dressed in rags;
was my dun suit:
can't figure out the mathematics:
marriage vows sealing the can:
those questions reeling in your ears:
"what if?" and
"but if?"

love stiffer than a starched shirt:
hawk! diva a rabbit to be his centrefold...

River at Waterloo

Can you breed me with our baby?
summer's a long ways behind and
winterwold is done,
comes a morning springtime should be
cuddlings with the sun;

y'know you haunt the bedroom,
I drink of the river in your eyes,
all night you're jealous with
deep suspicion of the day:
I'm sitting still to woo you sometimes...

All along the hedgerows
toasters are singing you a song;
the wind coos with deep affection,
the sky doesn't dare rain down:
should be party address your evergreens....

y'know you haunt the bedroom,
I'm spoke with the lovely in your eyes:
all day I'm jealous with
deep suspicion of the night:
I'm sitting still to woo you sometimes...

I'm not looking up to heaven to furnish me with signs,
I pray in joy and thank my blessings,
and hope you read in-between the lines:
should be like Wellington and Waterloo sometime...

River at Charing Cross

I can feel the breath of winter's fall...
early
here in the summer's leaf:
me, naked to my birthday suit...
walking by the river,

a tax on my speaking mouth: hurt by the choosing:
a love lost by her losing ways...

me,
naked to my birthday suit...
crossing the river,
all tides at a low ebb:
a love lost by her losing ways...

tax on my speaking mouth;
tax on my speaking mouth;
the sun waning by the river,
all tides at a low ebb:

walking by the river
watching couples holding hands...

me,
naked to my birthday suit:
wondering at the sun,
for,
there's no rain....
a love lost by her losing ways...

walking by the river
watching
couples the holding hands...

walking
by the river;
watching...

and the ships sail by...
I naked to my birthday suit...

I return home:
and my woman the marry me to herself...

River at Blackfriars

It's been clear
I've got to make it very clear
it's been a day,
a day mountain to past year...

Anyway it hurts,
a child clinging to your skirts;
anyway it hurts,
a child crying for deserts:
let's you and me divorce...

can I come to test the courts
marry, life a live-in death the course
what's the wanting worse:
let's you and me divorce...

River to a flood the need,
beggar to a banquet, greed,
fast to a famine, seed,
it'll to a nuclear fall-out lead....

River at London Bridge

And,
all my tears have flowed;
there shall be no longer a longer distance into dark;

and, both my eyes have dried:
the dark has conquered me never;

and, if all my wasted years
a wasteland turned,
I shall make of myself a wilderness of grass,
the desert into oasis turned...

and,
all my tears have flown:

and,
both my eyes have dried:
the hand that paid the piper
is mine:

I boat the river of my fortunes, alone;

my life was mortgaged
to a house that wasn't home:

I am a house that is my own...

River at West Ham

Heed fast the wounding of the heart,
those scar won't heal,
Its walls will tear down.

Heed fast the knocking of the pump,
that water is blood,
the blood will clot.

The hear the winding watch
sound a toll about the years you
wasted in a chest of drawers:

"It's heart dis-ease;
caused by the fat of wanting..."

"Wanting what?
"I was never wanting, but
my hands put by to mouth!"

Heed the warning knock!
Otherwise, be patient by the lack!

River at Greenwich

A knowing in the seed tells
time is clockwise to the birth of all seasons, and

a knowledge in the roots of man
is farmer to the bud
that harvests the sun and rain, and
reaches yonder towards the sky;

the sun and stars spirals out our fate,
which is to live destiny
to the far reaches of eternity:

and solace this:
the seed germinates;
man eats;
stars seek infinity:

the fire in each know
each its warm space,
and time, and each
grow to maturity:

a Big Love gives a time to each,
gives each a place in all this:

that Love knows a treason in each death.

River at Woolwich

A Greater Want shall close the door behind my back;
I shall to a greater home;
I shall to a farther sky.

No needs remonstrating behind my back,
and point the finger:
I wear Another's marriage ring;
I shan't be coming back.

And as I walk alone into the raving noon,
a shadow sits behind my back;
no needs for turning back:
I am rushing another River.

I gave, you gave me back,
but now no needs for giving back:
A loneliness waits for me lying where you are:
I go to a meeting beyond the river.

River at Gravesend

Would to kiss me sHe
with the petals of your mouth;
would wound me from the love of asking;

would meet me by my River's mouth
and kiss the day up until
come morning roundabout my ears;

would keep my company in profit,
harvesting the riches of old age:
would show me a Love that is capital;

would take the garlands of my life,
and toss it in my outpourings out to sea:
my life has met Your Love, and that was all its undertaking.

4. Anima Rising

**The last two days
of the Christ, retold**

Anima Rising

Contents

"0": Introduction............................

1. Prologue......................................
2. Leper House..............................
3. Inn...
4. Garden..
5. High-Priest House.....................
6. Pontius Pilate's House...............
7. In Praetorium Hall.....................
8. Golgotha....................................

Introduction

The poetry is a bare allegory of Christ's Good Thursday and Good Friday, a text based on the narrative of another text.

In Anima Rising, the writer. as 'god', is contradicted by the voices in the text as histories of suffering.

In the allegory, the Hell's Angel Christ's crucifixion is a sacrifice of the 'she' in him, the Anima, which it is argued is the human element in the Messiah, and thus human salvation through sacrifice in suffering. I believe, as many do, that the Christ lived and died a virgin; thus lived according to Law, as he never married...

Sexuality/sensuality is one of the themes of the dubpoetry, and one of links and lens to understanding in an attempt to show how I believe it to be central in all our lives...

The Form runs on a number of contradicting voices in the text, sometimes *another* interpretation of masculinity in the earlier parts, and later that of the Anima when she is becoming free-for-herself.

Each major structural part is made up of two major contradicting sections, and each of those two others in themselves.

Anima Rising, as a text, is to be seen as the fantasy of the writer/god that facilitates a reconciliation of Him with His world.

The images in the text are complex, especially as I don't always use simple metaphors, or anaematopia, but often construct a phrase or sentence so the meanings 'explode' in clusters and intentionally there must be several interpretations. This is a latter day influence on my poetry coming from French aesthetic theory. I do this to allow the reader to *write* meanings into the text; also have a choice of meaning, so that I as writer, and she/he are jointly constructing relationships: that is, *working* with words to produce a text. This is analogous to an element of free will...

Furthermore, no longer, as in my early years, influenced by the Imagists and Hans Magnus Enzensberger, I now believe that images must be *startling*! and a worthwhile text must be struggled with, and enjoyed again and again; as well as being 'written' too by the reader.

Thus, a lot of my images exists as French critic Roland Barthes explains, as *elisons* : meanings that you can just understand as a reader, and when held in the mind, they 'slip' and you have to work to make them plain...

Prologue - Barabbas!

"I am as starling in the night
the Night wears me as clothes in her heaven;
I am as silver in her raven hair:
Eve: once I spoke to she as Snake:
        sleeps me the Night,
        and in her gown
my dreams are as black holes starring...

As to her lips my stupor's kiss,
the dark side of moon's smile of crescent;
a lunatic is a face leering where
she looks: a shine into prison:
        Id in Ego,
        I am Shadow,
counsel more evil shade than Type...

Am I hawk in a dovecote you;
the Rage that drives vehicle of a wars;
the Death that bullies a canary you:
a lover is a bird of prey
        hater in you,
        I'm kind as claws:
I am to singing as is storms!

To a passion would speak his Name
|His love he sends: He in His called Heaven;
He's a Dream of Hope that would come my born
an opening space to thunder:
        lover-me do,
        I am you sends:
the Ugly Chat that is Eros,

beloved of a Life in breath,
and of a death That-mouth kissed onto mouth:
the Child that is forever Phoenix
and Place of Eternal Dead:
        son, a daughter
        of a wheel, both:
a Cycle in a Time a-dance

weather four seasons, sun in rain,
tickle to a chuckle to a mad laugh,
again; and again a silence in Night,
I: sleep to the scream of Being
              deafening to;
            also a shout
to raise roof of the house of bricks.

I for your storm's Eye a Palace,
no likes except a fan of butterfly,
liking your soul to orchids in a vase,
to an inner sky a sun set
              sapphire in pearl;
            and isthmus Night,
shall my star jacinth in your neck,

as wonderings to a seen scene
as much awes as put to a common place,
as mine as yours distance from a mirage:
holds the blindman a beggar-bowl within
              to this anguish;
            gaze amid Night
I'm rich with thee as one would choose.

Here's a love that would dare its say
even into a communion talks;
a Church where doings unto the Devil
as well as to the Myth of gods:
              goods in temple
            yet sins the host;
and prayers to the Primitive.

For flight to wings in empty air
is this day sky: there is a New that keeps,
holds treasure that radiates from the East,
flash of elder day's atomics
              is our fall-out
            fat from feast
from an old sky on old planet.

The New World now is breeding poor,
it has so many many that it lacks;
better rich the Old Man that knows his Brute
and sleeps in a bed of brute facts
              lives with plenty
            than a-plenty,
but knows that Night; and that Night Black...

There's a life comes another Death
missionary lives in Another's Love;
worships one: Another who wears His shoes
who sells the Third Deliverance:
 icing on cake
 the Merchant Bank:
tell me which murder is my choose?"

Gospel according to Mark

His time was near, his climax into a storm: the way was clear.
At Simon the leper's house, a woman he knew, cloud in her head he knew, poured expensive oil onto his crown - there was fault: those present said it was at fault: "It could have fed the poor!"
"But the poor are always here.... She has made me ready for over standing there..."

Part One: Leper House

I- i

I am the lion and roar sun
and the sheer shun of the snow down
and welcoming winsome
              a kiss to you
with you and lovingly listen to you
              and boo!
and frown upon a clown face too.

Love-eyes with the smiling to you
straight-through and all-new come to you
may the morning matter
              sing all evening
for you, for you a celebration ring
              and bring!
may life gift you a real something.

Shall I the solemn silence sing
rally roo with a rhythmic ring
eager all to echo
              and too in tune
to be this life with baton worn as plume
              and croon!
is sung my sing-song sat in room.

So certainly my round the moon
my circling too Whoever Whom
mine the grasp of Heaven
              and kowtow sun
the white noise of applauding stars become
              well done!
for the won game going for one.

I the kinsman of the star-crossed shade
I darkness, I am the bonny sun
sitting on a chamberpot I made
loud and handsome O my father's fruit:
peace me you in the tidings secret
tower me my Master and divine
how riches have I, yet I token
power I, down-wind devious sea.

Shall you music liddy lady-room?

*I am an Ancient and I new bloom
I ask to sally further the-sky-
-has-fallen to the fetch of your shade:
shall I drowse the demon questioning...*

*I kinsman of the whinging grave
the dread for coward-into-coffin
- O drown me from my break-wave Asker
guilty me from my branching off limb
for I am spoken to be Saver-
-Sung-to-Thee though questioning times-Noon
and why: why the pistol-broken night?*

*"Look you at the season winter
the scab that would be life is scar;
would kiss you leper for better
- yet know your lover thus as <u>you</u> are!"*

*(Follow me your master!
"Shall you save me?"
Yes and answer!
"and my brick house?"
Let the Landlord deliver!
"And wife?"
Care not! be burning-leaver!
"leave?"
Hell rather?)*

*Why the whip-lashed-lightning-cracked of night
and the soap-sud foam of mad-dog mouth?
would I be snoring mind, and rather
would the whisper-of not this cancer!*

I- ii

Die effervescent fire!
for the cake is mud
and ballet though the doing
loving comes to grave:
fire fire fire!
-die good.

Dare the Devil drink you!
water is too wet
if eyes drop, chaste with acid
brag you poison mum:
live faster!
-die good.

Don't romance a darling!
kiss adder and asp
 if she love-bites bite her back
bees sip, stings wise wasp:
love larger!
-die good.

A last would I rather shine of shoes
sure-stepped on step in step-on-air and
live long, lover-long-lived-with with me
for this care is after a fashion
 gravity stuck solid down-to-earth:
a last word vanishes day to night.

Under the silk-sheet-lover no room!
is her sitting-down-to-table feast
enough gentling of a ghost to babes
lastly seduces she mine as will:
a tenderness loves the speech of kiss
at last the whirl world ends listening.

(A miracle enough!
"This glance of fingers?"
Feel you spark?
"master - this heat?"
Feel your love living!
"Does my rib-bone erect?"
Feel heavenly?)

*Sigh with sympathy where suckles wind
where cuckoo's calling recollects spring,
if you would lover, love her garden
and her blossom-bud; she doubles bed
your fancy goes galloping with herd;
if wants recall wonder, love tender...
passion's hymn plucks punishment out words.*

I- iii

I!!

*Never till want breast-bone-borrowed Eve
was less-than-Perfect Adam; then man
then conversation of the cuddling:
this breath is more than one; at least two:
one's desperation coupling desire*

*and we waste fire working matchless wood
for life is the polishing to shine:
and as life's furniture shapes from tree
mine is chip off the carpenter's block.*

*(Be leprosy!
"And the hurt?"
Cut off limb!
"and respect?"
Look to lepers!
"Will I wife?"
Wouldst save all?)*

*Never the one-blood breed an estate
the sole-lonely yet twin understand
the one man kiss fingers tasting lips,
one love: and one so trumpet one grand...*

II- 1. i

Night drips in dusk
nice as my pen-nib swells
as spoke into the sponge of paper sucks,
nibbles into ink wells
the writing tells
of night hung on a moon at tusk.

Dark-night-sometimes
wears sometime-yellow rags
some of the moon's shine summers her sometimes
with gold the sun day robs,
the golden flags
love-looks at summer's-day-sometimes.

And night warming
as moon captures sun ways
rays striptease into naked returning
night into blushes blaze,
moon's wax waylays
dawn drizzling day - oh!: morning!

ii

*If I was your kind-and-country
cook-into-olive-oil,
would the pot make the pigeon broil
would your taste take a fancy
more than the one time?
-fiancee?*

*If I was your lady-looking
-milk-made-and-marriage-maid,
would the Prince put me on parade
would you think me good-looking
once more than sometimes?
-your girlfriend?*

*If I was your holy-worship
-woman-with-given-Spark,
would you desire me as your Ark
would you come to my service
once and for all time?
-wouldst love me?*

II- 2. i

Should tongue diet
live a voice fasting self?
food is what the mouth wants on the quiet
put hunger on the shelf
one loves oneself:
put fire and finger into fat!

Whose shame say 'can'ts'?
fat is to taste of Love
flesh is what the cake-and-cherry-world wants
life has so little of,
do what size does
and shame those who devil us: 'can'ts'.

Eat and let live
make the taste-buds riot
pork give, give bacon, make the stomach give
don't give-in to diet:
since man eats fat
why so you think that repulsive?

ii

Was I your hug-and-apple-pie
sink-into-an-apron,
would my strings be your scaffold strung
my smile there to make you try
would you love always?
-live in me?

And if I your payfling-and-fight
rival-soldier-in-arms,
would I to doll to pick up charms
be chubby your little light
yours always always?
-inside me?

If I was your gold-and-wed-ring
kiss-on-to-cushion-him,
would I just wearer of purse string
stranger-loved with whom lived-in:
one's lover always?
-love in me?

II- 3. i

Love or life dies
live mouth against a kiss
even if the stars fall hearts shall shout skies
sun in shine shall be bliss
hail-storm amiss
won't warry weather with the windrush rise

and conquer this:
love is but bare second
a moment in a turning round to kiss
shall a finger beckon
love to reckon,
dues paid for such credited bliss.

Heed thus on end
how silenced heart is free
how stone open-heart surgery can mend:
can stained heart welcome me
your lover be
your love-friend more than your girlfriend?

ii

*If I was your all-out-war-friend
brother-in-law-in-arms,
would you stick to me through these storms
would our love come to an end
would you kill so still?
-and in love?*

*If I was your union-at-work
comrade-in-uniform,
would you rally to me each morn
strike a light even though broke
would you weary still?
-friend and love?*

*If I was your carpenter's mate
married-man-to-the-wood,
would you share with me bread and blood
or tinder me your ungrate
would you cross so still?
-and beloved?*

Gospel according to Mark

**His time was near, his climax into a storm: the way was near...
It was the Passover spent at an inn in Jerusalem: he took his twelve
with him, bathed he them and then they ate, dipped bread in one
plate: he said: "One man here will betray, one man be betrayed.
Things must come to an end..."**

Part two:
Inn

I- 1. i

   There is life
  but consider the sky
  and the Dreamer who wakes;
Love, I sleep on a bed of knives
  pity-please bless my eyes
the lens of the camera weeps
  water thirsting in me

   I would know
  Thy skin, Thy colour eyes
  whether Thy breasts are firm
though I know Yours have milk enough
  is that sweet substance white?
the dummy of the infant lacks
  cream tasting in me

   I love Thee
  love Thee as my living
  show me Your shape of mouth;
though I am married to Your voice
  love speaks as parable
my talking love does not inform:
  I only know I die!

   Shall fever
  shall forehead noon due Sun
  Summer-You in all days,
dark of night Thy delivered sleep
  the gauda moon Thy fame
and the sparkling stars Thy worship:
  but need I more than Name!

   I am male
  would worship You with kiss
  yield even unto skin
woo You with ecstasy of 'yes'!
  -but married remove veil
enter communion with skin:
  I need Thy blood and flesh!...

I- 1. ii

        Thou living,
    loving idiot me
    orders reparation
a forgiving for the sinning
        causing wrath of Angels;
Who is Cloth of Many Colours
        wants murdering of one...

        Coloured red
    Thou tribe hunting bison
    hugged wedded to land
that dowry so taxed and stolen
    so little was reserved;
redcoat-bloody was red sunset
        -my flesh has done Thee wrong

        Coloured black
    Thou dancer's feet enchained
    and refused their birthright;
dancer's child matured with a will
    to inherit refuse:
a debt to this estate remains
        -my flesh has done Thee wrong

        Yellow talc
    Thou tinted ancient time
    waxed candle before flames
raised by me; I raised you drunken
    fed you poisoned stupor
greed reined golden reign to ruin
        -my flesh has done Thee wrong:

        Thou living
    Lover of all that's Light
    also embrace in kiss
all from Garden that light ruins:
    I, also those I kick:
thus says Cloth of Many Colours:
        -my flesh must pay for wrong!

I- 2. i

        In the raw
     we own so many wives
      many men many wombs
other than to that fixed as star
       leave me my teeth in jaw:
I would age and to death with One
      Who suffers me to last

        I am he
    who cripples up with pain
     who gathers chest to grief;
both as beggar who begs to weep
      and child too cried out dream:
sleep I and ravished in one bed
     -the One-Life makes us same

        As I live
     my living is a hope
      for here and hereafter
is thieving from the Dark of God
       and promise to a child:
my life mentions Man to Chaos
      I hurt Most with my death

        And to die
    is victim the most proud
     to share a martyr's Fate
welcoming to blood-heritage
      last vote of democrat
rising to star with the first life:
      each dying equals death

        Is a death
    and a shrink of Heaven
     the salt rubbed in to scar
the poison with a loving look,
      suffer each as you are:
torturer too and tormentor
      ride you beast of burden...

I- 2. ii

        You know All
    the little dwells with Large
    teacher-mine mind me Law:
"All Life has but moments to keep
    riches is all conceit
true gold lies in love one-to-one."
    -I must share all with All

    all-in-all
    the same is all in All
    no-one richer special
though some one's house is on the hill
    it's castle-in-an-air
the poor-house a Loved-One loves still:
    life's a bridge built in All

    going gone
    is auction of all life
    a steal of fat finger
I have not made the bidding fair:
    richer raised fore-finger
high cost living I keep for keeps
    keeps wife and sprat what lean

    In whether
    I am a Midas touched
    vivid with waste of it,
this counting petty-cash of lives,
    whether a spend-thrift life,
depends on the charge and change back:
    is my suffering tax

    and know All:
    must I my all to All
    that or the loss of All;
and was I but a maudlin man
    this all would be little
-All this charity is worth: is
    a living, most of all...

II- 1. i

The street are killed with dragon corps
dragging two wheels worn on a wire and
also lives on hire
I am the highway fox
due darling you to retire

can you smell the sex of the heat
eating men contemplating death and
hot ones out of the net
I kiss the sexy road
love like you hung my neck

- nearly broke my neck on the turn
returning my raving to rest and
next to never the nest
I ride high joy tonight
Pandora - bare your chest!

Do you watch mac-in-tyre?
remember I retire?
mighty men may crash
saw his future flash?
life: find him a buyer!
Woman love me now on the street
on the concrete
make me raw combustion by fire!

Angel you;
piston have you
ball-bearing too,
and a charge for sparking:
oiled, this engine has come to you

rider on rail
engine begun,
with licence for driving:
 drive me like a bullet from a gun.

The rocket horse is whinny thing
a-sing something cuts down road's throat and
the racket hits right notes
I hum some same something
Pandora listens both
the orchestration owes the night;
sight seduces stuttering stars and
blood drunks drinkers on bar
-come eat me Pandora

speed and my Angel war!

I'll play you like guitar
race you like racing-car
do you a fast deal
put you nose to wheel
to heaven in my car!
Woman, I'll love you in the street
on the concrete
put racing circuit where you are!

Driving teacher
mechanic too,
a master of his tools:
my whole career is down to you.

This apprentice
scholarship won,
asks practice in your school:
teach her a lesson by your tongue.

The streets are killed with dragon corps
dragging two wheels worn on a wire and
also lives on hire
I am the highway fox
due darling you to retire

rev me woman higher
make combustible fire!
mighty men may crash
see my future flash,
life: spark in my wire!
Woman I'll love you in the street
on the concrete
wear you down just like my tyre!

II- 1. ii

Lover was our April days
lather to our razor;
near-sharp as the axe-blade
winter, and was our together,
the ice-cut breathe-weather;

and the charm of a blossoming sun,
new-looks to fashioning leaves,
toasts from the sky well-done
the toddling chalk-hill down
down all through
      the widening
           door of day,
till born boy-baby rams
bring all to a bounce
begging to bargain butts and
mothers answer you
May!

April-you was my raincoat;
a want on a rain-day wore you
till splash! of the sun's moult
merried in a mine of silver suit.
May I love again as I did you.

II- 2. i

We are as following to daily star
in circles to a planet are,
looking to a blue sky
but crowded under clouds.

Mountains are summonses to climb to suns
course to a coast-line runs,
a vastness is the sea
stands each land on water

and comes the sombre and the shilling moon
the rage! rage! of passed-over noon,
misery afternoon
 a gloom of an evening.

II- 2. ii

As supper is one sitting down to course
shall we savour a little sauce,
eat on a hearty heart
due payments give the bill.

Eat!: for shall a butcher reap all for shelf
eat, and eat plenty: help yourself,
eat Heaven out of Hell-
eat!: and kosher food eat-

my blood is claret, my flesh a biscuit
darling shall I a seconds kiss
and my live breath feed you
Life to an open mouth.

Gospel according to Mark

There was a Garden. He prayed to God to make pardon. His friends took to sleep: "One," He said, "before this night crows out of its keep, will deny my keep..."
Then with a kiss came Judas to betray: in anger a friend cut off a soldier's ear. The man he cared was else: "He that cuts," He said, shall cut himself...."

Part Three:
Garden

I- 1. i

Growing sung that which is wonderful fire
that listening to melody of sky
some pipers on orchestras of wind fly
too: kingfishers swallowing fire.
Is that a piano that strums his wire?
Or impossible blue heaven of sky?
Bliss is a song a musician must fly
to: life's a tightrope, must one love the wire!
Yesterday came piper to raise a flute
to meet with lips after the winter's send
this is wind on the wing blue sky of youth
this kiss young-looks, love-looks, swells love-friend
       then drips the ripen juices of the fruit:
       again!: all in harvest comes to an end.

I- 1. ii

I to this springtime come bee stinging wine
hurt of ache that follows hurricane blind
the want, having; to do, but no incline
and the would waits as a longing to mind.
Flower to this sty come as heaven scent
passenger to passing the perfume went
as a season to loving living lent:
flowers for a garland the Garden meant.
O for a passion that flowers as fire!
that holds hands with heaven as bears the chest,
but holding hands is holding hands to eye
closing as opening Pandora's chest:
       would that I came to this crossing with sleep,
       each time I know I close my eyes, I weep.

I- 2. i

Father in fire, mother aflame to match
mesh of this machinery soldered I
soldier of flames fetched from a flame to match,
familiar of mechanics I die:
I, weaver's embroidery, those two's thatch,
sewing, stitching, knitting: together's sigh
wonder of woman-man's two-timing watch
jointly two-faced Heaven and Earth: one why.
I material two, am heavenly
You: too my liking to a doting snake;
from the instant of a spark to that tree
You: unlike as did worm in apple make:
> Heaven there and Hell, unworldly here: me,
> blissing stomach-full, also this dull ache.

I- 2. ii

Eye to I, shine into ink I-to-I:
to thought as mind microscope into dark
as light into space, a magnetic spark
as hesitating night is sun to sky?
Am One alone, manufacturer I:
roves factory to a dream of One's walk
loud speaker to echo of One's-own talk
Tailor whose fabric is the asking why?
And never river joining with some stream
never branch stemming into other limb
never parts: ecstasy awaiting seam:
never you, thou - we, never her nor him:
> *and all's to a play featuring 'just the same',*
> *I am You, to know by another name?*

II- 1. i

Dreamer me writer out on a wire
'God', he's whiplashed snake, ache in earthquake
I'm his signature, road tied to tyre
his Ghost's amuse: Heaven and Hell his make.
As can his wordy love inkling of fire
I am subject to his noun 'I' awake,
messenger to his fact: fiction entire:
I am the passions that his music wake.
Part am I painter, piece in my painting
hero am I, nagging thorn in his crown
given am I, yet a jigsaw wanting
drawn by strokes to a point, never full-blown
    yet figure fashioned to have a faith in
    I'm a creature that's infant that's full grown.

II- 1. ii

Great macho god goading machine
might muscled to preen:
man, I'm more than a sheen
more than quill than word
much more than breeding you've seen
on the crouch on couch of machine:
I'm a fledgling bird
she: typed-in-you thing.

And as you are feathering wing
to your gathering
shall be clutch of hurricane wind
the loose sky a fall
and the map of stars no inkling
of bad Fate: a bewildering
balance shall recall
you: should nest-egg warm.

Rise to the spilling sunsplash dawn
rosy-apple morn
lightening looks upon our lawn
gardening out house
if ever shall you allow born
conversation with femaled, scorn
in your manner-house:
shall live-in love free...

II- 2. i

Highways are sentences of in-come tax
written narratives of punishing dies
jammed types of a Writer borrowing facts,
only the last word is sign for one's eyes.
Dreamer me Writer out on a wire
'God': man's his match: magician writing fire
a-fire pen, pointing Babel to higher
hire of week's-work-reach to weekend retire.
A life am I living, fiction in fact
God is my writer, I', part-child of God
a Muse meant me to be shuffled by pack,
narrative is my suffering at odds:
        words am I on the page of my Writer
        real am I a part from my Creator.

II- 2. ii

I, second in thee
oh - a dam in cloud -
I, second in thee,
an upturned table asking why-
-pleading seconds,
I second in thee:

yes,
the prayer
yes:

no! to the care-less
        dangling of the cordless
              hawk busy buying
                      business built in air
                              biding for the by-and-by
                                  bye-bye:

yes:
waking the watch
to prayer
yes!

I, second in thee
second in thee:

no,
the lost ear
no:

yes! to the love-kiss
        and the meet with marry bliss
                and to rather listening
                        than hit-and-miss,
                                yes! to this
                                        that than
Judas...

Gospel according to Mark

Took He to a trial: tried they false-witness; his disciple bore false witness. The trial decided He understood death...

Part Four:
High Priest House

I- 1. i

And the darkness bleeds
my purple cloth of woe:
"Sheds shine as summer seeds:
Go!
you are bared skin
you are bared skin."

Spills an empty glass
ghosts taste of the toasting well:
"You drink of future-passed:
Tell!
you are a river
you are a river."

Prisons as dropped stone
winged far from wonder why:
"Breaks hallowed bed of bone:
Die!
you are a sky
you are a sky!"

I- 1. ii

Pity-pray the Raging Bull that Gods:
may the blind stars and one-eyed sun
be ever-guided by ones who
      see clearly with vision of sky
      hear loudly with stereo of love
      and feel with the past pain culture
      of their inner and outer skin!

I- 2. i

I try trigger ten-finger touch
both eyes, full mouth of lips
both arm bare in the bear-hug, but
body banished bit in thee,
dead in the dying-done
born, body banished but in thee
I'm bare to thee: no false witness.

I'm true to trembling trumpet
waltz with the winding waist,
mathematic my music mouth
signature in sound for thee
tune in the tuning-fork
tone, signalling sign to thee
near note to thee: no false witness.

I- 2. i

Especially as darling dare
to breathe me song,
I want you singing;
and song-you sung
will be as me in a warble-me
I in a summer suit:
breath in me,
breathing:

burn before you bury me brother to me:
I beg you bear me true witness...

Especially as tomorrow
tongues tight to a crow
cock-a-doodle, do
the dawn-days drip
like drops of light in a puddle-night
I a pyjama rise
riddle-me,
waking:

eat earth ever you exit me off this Earth:
I beg you bear me true witness...

II- 1. i

Down darkness down;
due to the shark-fin moon
only a grey wool knit the beard of night
a whisper of cloud
and drippings of stars:
now! and then only the shadow of doubt
the basking shark rules...

Anyway: gloom
and any way escapes
the razor-sharp of the saw-tooth light, dark
dribbles over lips
slashed by the light shark:
blood! and only the blood of the ink-black
drip the gloom of death...

here and hour
now, and the witness-box
and the clever of the shadow-boxing night
punch-drunk grabs grappler
holding onto win:
rings! only the knell of the last knoll knows
the lose-funeral.

Drops dreadful drown;
ghostly with the Word-Love
only dark dungeons denies the glow-worm
glut creating fire,
arcs adder to asp-
asks! but to bite mightier than sword asks:
my love of Word kings.

Wordy write me
right hand worthy right me
extension to the suffering of Muse
point of fore-finger
part in the paper,
print! folk of a fertile blue-printed yolk:
brood of Your pen's lay.

Love and lovely
He laughs the loud listen
to the bells tolling of the future plot;
Magic and Righter
He frowns as my task:
tell! only told is your demand in deal,
not like to hero...

Done darkness down
dawn a distant downpour;
this night develops as a negative.
am I broke in sleep
am I woke in dream:
now! am I now only a photograph
a process into dark

anyway: gloom
night answering my ask
with a show of stars, none about to fall
once fallen marbles,
clusters from rain-clouds,
wets! a priceless sprinkling of sparkling wets
miserly on grass:

O! my care sun
my care for shine with-child;
toys wish for penny-and-blue-ribbon sky
baked bun for bared back
joy a sting ray-bright,
day! livelong sweltering of mad-dog day,
noon such hot nonesuch

and love-looks like
outcast the mask of night.
Day could be the countenance of grimace,
night same, marks with scar
scares by changing face,
dark! chameleon with the warping dark:
day bares to raw skin.

I this gloom-thing
once again would summer
be fledgling for flight far-flung of feather
fatting with season,
love-looks to skyward,
sun! and only a merry-weather sun:
peace with its witness...

II- 1. ii

Why-
and a riddle-me why
my rider:
why you pucker-brow-up and thump-chest,
why?

and sad-eye
send with the sorrow-sigh
and cry,
why my rider why?

ask I:
is lie?
have you reason-die?
or fly you with the may-fly bye-bye?
-can't eye can I.

Why?
won't you solid tree trunk buried
      girth in earth
dig depth in dirt
silent with the sickle slash hurt?
aren't you not made man by birth?

-why?

II- 2. i

Down darkness drown;
this night is an ocean
and the torrents of silence is its flood
time makes a river,
dream is island-place:
land! I am foreigner without country
nightmares storm with noise:

am I the last waker
      drowned by this
           'shush' of voice...

Sleep! were I asleep
she would be my cushion,
rest her heart's peace, her breasts a chest of dreams,
her kiss closet to eyes
clothes her touch in love:
sleep! if a 'He' Father-Gods in Heaven
she's Man kind on Earth:

Word, praise woman that is
      a half of talk
           in me...

II- 2. ii

Why-
art shy?
my rider want beddy-by
He writes of lady-land lie?
buy! Boy, buy!

Why, you cry?

Sweet
eternal friend
make my love end:
say your rich love begins...

I give him ecstasy
he torments
me, calls me
'nasty'! -
oh! he worships me! says:
"You're an ugly dog in the frigid wind!"
he means this mad dog in heat sends

*sweet eternal friend
make my love end:
say your rich love begins...*

*he
calls himself boss
his life is worse
without me, says I'm curse:
oh! I'm Heaven here on Earth and champagne wine!
he's the sun:
but sun sets, someone must see you shine!*

*sweet eternal friend
make my love end:
say your rich love begins...*

*You know
I despise myself
for my loathsome love that someone else
who is living power over and above me,
yet admire me
for my nature's superb
as I suffer in this spiteful world:*

*sweet
eternal Rift
we live a myth:
this myth contradicts,
we must find a synthesis-*

*our conclusion is nice:
SACRIFICE!*

Gospel according to Mark

One washed hands: and was released a dark side: Barabbas!

Part Five:
Pontius Pilate's House

One: I- 1. i

Dawn jumps and as a spoken song-bird shouts,
the bed of my room's ceiling is blues wrung
sky is stretched cord hanging the bulb of sun,
I, winter's to the new of old day's out.
I, a lean to my leaning mountain, doubt
the marriage of the inner mountain drum
to veil of glad tidings that's tied its tongue
never speaks in me who has found it out.
Speechless, like a cuckoo sits darkling night
breast broody on the lay of nest-egg sun
all voices flights an asking, dark dims light
more empty shelled, never cracked, wise owl come:
        comes stranger sometimes chorusing in flight:
        a heart and dawn leaps to hear Singer sung.

One: I. 1. ii

A whisper of Louder Echoes is sing
of a sudden song-bird settled a sit,
small chord of One Harmony marking with
witness with the whistling of small hymn,
once heard one compares Greater Listening
to the world's wordier manuscript writ
one no longer doubts, by a Greater Wit
than child worshipping one word praising Him.
As can skyward sing to a sounding sky,
so can serpent in the slime-sand same thing
swell swinging on the bell-ropes all a-ring:
this chorus in the cathedral is My:
        choir to the mirroring-Me on Earth:
        same worth is serpent and singer; sky; dirt.

One: II- 1.
  i

A love-land and a new day courts
I am morning beloving with a sun
I am the arriving to a stillness
crossing over the light day melts.

Breaking fast with the Eastern eye
the bruise of you is hurt of hurricane
marrying to my moor-lands dark-due-he;
feast on my spread come morning-due:

lips to a taste romance the juice
spilling over tongue gargling down the throat
-a few love-lines living are left to night,
somehow farewell climax a toast.

Darling, doubtless I'm a tall pride,
mountain to dust, a tall pride leaves no doubt
that right arm is on shoulder with the left:
in me it's the love of you prouds.

And as I fetch to me this calm
a flower-bud blossoms as unravels,
"Would you want to be a worm at its heart?"
I am stillness; you are a storm...

  ii

A storm to your down day clusters
now: I am spread beneath the arch of moon
asleep; asleep to the sky and dark sun,
still: still you gather cloud to rain

heavy rain, shall rain forty days?
but now a storm is a lover loved still
and hugged; because you pleased me, give! and gave;
and loving giver give away.

  iii

A tongue for my maid mouth tasting,
this gentle of a candlelight to night,
I would a moth to wax with love-waxed love
die Icarus in flight to flame

now sleep: now joy in knot asleep
nor day nor dream part like dark into light.
But light into dark, awake and broke fast,
breakfast in garden; wash of hands...

iv

Shall loving giver give away?
Father-worship, release the bride to groom
alone a head of house and home remain?
Shall loving giver give away?

v

Away was I a road route child
trained and roller-coaster ride to suit
waistcoat you and the slap of a ruler-
male, "Sorry-thank-you-pardon-Sir,

"and-praise-be-God-was-a-boy-child."
Lover made you in me: scar in your bed;
-now I'm redneck and pussy-footed free,
lover-you tied to by the neck.

God gave woman, love give me breath
give me myself, I'm bone tied to your chest!
and comfort-come's wreckage in an alley
blind-bluff down one-way one-man's street.

God gave you man, man give release
your Mama was mortal, I'm that maid half
man learn that lesson written in your genes:
live-in love lover give away?

vi

I would kiss as marauding flirt
one eye on the flavour of morrow's lips;
yet would your loved-one this lover love still
for still is nakedness to night.

A near night nourishes my star
and names my nature with my signature;
as so I ebbed low with the tides of dawn,
so shall I vanquish as the eve...

One: II- 2.
i

Now sleep like a sheep gathers wool
and a knit of cardigan as of dreams;
you come blaze of a neon city eyes:
Barabbas-twinned; electric; light

a barb of lightning knifing night
and delight; and a muscle of the 'he might'
buttocks tight; tanned; dressed in the leather-right.
This crossroads comes a wash of hands...

ii

Never more the wrestling love make
never, never, never more kissed with priest
high-priest of strangling with his rope love: cured,
cured my skin of this night's fever,

epilepsy due the shine moon,
shall fever in forehead new noon be sun
I new fitness outside drug dependence;
I that still night to bed in sleep.

iii

Writer: I am that ebony-She:
culture of Your country-Israel root;
Thou hast missed-laid me on Your passage roam:
I now leave You chalk from blackboard

leave You love-less in a sentence.
Am i a pronoun that will new word
new capital in capital letters;
be Subject to an active verb.

iv

Are You a Voice inked into storm
a calling to the four winds hacked through sky
over land that wears white with black water,
all in a world led by Your Name.

And am I but a suffering,
but a task for a writing down to tell;
I am mentioned me due Your choice of pen,
Your choice words choose that the-I die.

v

I'm in You, I'm the woken dark
outside sleep printed public in the hall,
a beggar in this almshouse by trade,
that merchant beggar of the soul,

self-same thief in the asylum,
ghost-catcher of the child due for a fall
and the watch-over, and the confessor:
I'm grave-robber: no body else...

vi

Age-eyes with the clouding has me,
night's spectre-to is of fact going ghost;
none ever youth dream the burden bent back:
I am wearing that spectacle.

My 'hello' no longer novels
my write comes to a sign by my Writer,
youth is to be filled in with a full-stop,
the last 'i' is a head of dot.

Two: I- 1.
i

I am a noise
in a weepy-me in a geyser heart
the boreholes of blood rush to fountain-head
and coagulates the sun in shine-day
flagging fine-weather fare in a fair sky:
still, am I noise
in news-stand nattering and in facade;

I surrender you
in a quiet place,
in a quiet place my love is a bird-song for you...

Yet am I scream
and a shouting-me in a sorry hat
hating the eclipse of the night-shade moon
to the maiden-noon of the mellow sun
a following with fledgling flight for fire:
alone and scream
I am nonsense type with water tap;

I surrender you
in a quiet place,
in a quiet place my love is a bird-song for you...

ii

Should be singing:
mine and a made-to-be-mine morrow's day
ah! but adventure comes children to child
we are future followings to this flood,
my Father to the fetching features me,
mother to my:
rain-day, milk-day, wean-to-wedding-day wear:

I surrender to you
in a quiet space,
in a quiet space my love is a bird-song singing for you.

... all day through year,
and a New Year is She through this new wear,
sleeps our child secure in a swaddling wrap
welcome is the seat in Fathering lap;
so shall a question in this chorus rap
brothers-to-me
as those sounding to me sistering choir:

I surrender to you
in a quiet space,
in a quiet space my love is a bird-song singing for you.

Two: II- 2.
i

*In my still, born of a quiet
palace of places, theres my woman,
daughter of one and all other ways,
milk-mead of the slivering:
I: mother of an eye in the hurricane-day,*

*dear darling of peaceful-have-you
cuddling from the crush-of-the-creature-world
Madonna of the fuse of a smile,
and a kiss and 'I love you':
I: I the miser to self in broody hen coop;*

*now's yet another sacrifice:
death: perhaps a last put-to-sleep of heart:
death: a last 'wait'! to the acher-heart:
after, a Wake to wake heart:
I and my heart a place of castle from the storms.*

ii

*It was my guilt in innocence
and my lone star hauled by a following
brought me to this flood and this fire,
Hell and eye-water, danger:
death in this season of calling by the cuckoo.*

*Love stole me from my inner pain
became embodied in your style, your kin
yet you robbed words tasted by my tongue
a pain filled where love came from:
 my death has no more aching echo than your name.*

*I shall survive, as peace survive:
there is safe inside an immortal book
forever pages my passion prints,
Heaven resides my reader:
death is a censorship of me: my life-story...*

Gospel according to Mark

In Praetorium Hall they mocked him; took off his crown in putting on a crown; and did beat...

Part Six:
In Praetorium Hall

I- 1.
i

I, now my scarecrow jaundice, no
the yes-man, no the stabber-hawk
that dares down the dead-end dally,
no now my fit of the frighten,
no a rally to robbery
no! to the clenched fist for sake end
no! to a blindfold in case in
case of seeing; in case rue in.
Yes. To the fret of forgiving
one loudly oath of the willing,
one soothing kiss to the sighing
and sickening: the reasoning
      to the yellow of the wax-love:
      hurt heart to settle in me still.

ii

I, yes my cushion-caring, know
murder no gorilla raw fist
no! appointment to poison no
cuttle-fish in the dinner-dish
no! bull-whipped in the bull-ring, no!
and no! a death-wish to the sick
no! those voodoo who do pin-prick
and pick up the beating-stick - no!
Perhaps? - no perhaps: here heed to
die rather than yes listen to,
you, and all passengers you-to:
shall hesitate and a kiss blow
      cuddle-to to kow-tow, to heal
      better shall - or shock kill me still!

I- 1.

i

A quiet heart would rage,
       a rose heart stone.
a volcano's heart to heart of quick-fire!
... but there is a still heart sleeps

a temple in a crown
       that knows its King,
a purple quilt that's rest unto a Prince:
this dark is but an asleep

a dreaming in a part
       inside the Id:
a mare that bolts ridden astride by night:
this story is my mind's sleep:

an unconscious to rage
       to quiet heart
that gallops beneath the whip of night still:
still as this page is Writer...

ii

What wonders has the |Mind
       that dreams of things
never has, but ever is a ghost
captured in a frame of mind,

of sleep: a project of lens
       in bone and lantern
that would image Him to a place He Kings
inside out his own black-box.

Forever is a Prince
       a Magician,
here in a Land pays tribute to Caesars
ever as killed its Maker.

And as the Ever-Child
       on its thumb sleeps,
ever invitation to a murder
as the Murderer is dreams.

II. 1. i

With root in the roo of the rooster's crow
broody hen to lay,
is a hen like a rooster down to lay

amongst the flat and flatten a-bed
downwards from a sky;
and with-wings a wonder is to sky

is to fever a fashion of sky,
a quieting glide
down down the riding of a whirling glide

-cock with a whoop would hurrah! such a sky
that sends him such dawn:
same chorus lays the broody hen to dawn

-I'm a knot in the tie of a lover-love-you
my loved-one, can fly me do?

II- 1. ii

Is He Drummer to the due on the day
Drum-roll to the night's wane:
the wax of the sun to the night-time's wane

a sky enough for the clouds to be in,
wanting to be rain;
and a gather to the eye-lids of rain

a swashbuckle in the belt of storm-wind
belching out the air;
the bellow to this bellowing of air

-the flash! of a karate-kick of sky:
lightening to storms:
is He that marching of a day through storms

-I'm a thread through the eye of a needle-need-You
The-Loved-One, can storms me do?

II- 2. i

Nakedly mortal, so a flesh of thorns
I, as mine, from first jagged edge of horn
to transcendental, blooming of the rose

Death comes from fever, fever from a kiss
the vice of lips to lockjaw to disease
death: life-living-everlasting after

death: life is a female and male sex:
the beauty of a her and him-self:
in two, the becomings of making one,

as-one dream of bed made into marriage,
an act become Communion by two:
life spark into becoming one from two.

II- 2. ii

Nakedly mortal, therefore kissed to Death,
I, as they under that thorny-bush cloud
-but Breath blessed by the bleeding there of rose-

come through this day as come through wind beating:
with all-weather wear wrapped about our hug;
but lest a love lost leaning us from Night.

In spring, I and mine, we egg the cuckoo
lain in another's nest; come summer fly
and fat in autumn; winter, leave roost to rest,

sleep in a bed of all our yesterdays:
so shall a Dreaming of tomorrow's spoils
wake with us from the Dark to today-light?

Gospel according to Mark

Was He crucified...

Part Seven:
Golgotha

To a sleep shall I on a two-thief hill:
thief, Him the Writer, He the written love:
myself the she-is-been,
the two-in-one to both:
'herself' in Manner ghost
and 'He the Man', a Ghost:
I'm a Father, a Mother, two;
suffering the third Cross
in-spires-us, a Church
as a Guide and a Save promised
promises the Love-still;
still fingers this crossed heart

He wrote...

---

www.ingramcontent.com/pod-product-compliance
Ingram Content Group UK Ltd.
Pitfield, Milton Keynes, MK11 3LW, UK
UKHW041435180426
11947UKWH00007B/457